JOSEPH
AND HIS
COAT of MANY COLORS

25 Years of Magical Reading

ALADDIN PAPERBACKS
EST. 1972

First Aladdin Paperbacks Edition, 1997

Aladdin Paperbacks
An imprint of Simon & Schuster Children's Publishing Division
1230 Avenue of the Americas
New York, NY 10020

Also available in a Simon & Schuster Books for Young Readers
Edition.

The text of this book was set in Utopia.
Printed and bound in the United States of America.

10 9 8 7 6 5 4 3 2 1

The Library of Congress has cataloged the Simon & Schuster Books
for Young Readers Edition as follows:
Kassirer, Sue.
Joseph and his coat of many colors / retold by Sue Kassirer;
illustrated by Danuta Jarecka.
p.   cm.
Summary: After being sold into slavery in Egypt by his jealous
brothers, Joseph becomes an important man and is able to come
to his family's rescue during a famine.
ISBN 0-689-81227-2 (hardcover).—ISBN 0-689-81226-4 (pbk)
1. Joseph (Son of Jacob)—Juvenile literature. 2. Bible stories, English—
O. T. Genesis—Juvenile literature. [1. Joseph (Son of Jacob) 2. Bible
stories—O. T.] I. Jarecka, Danuta, ill. II. Title.
BS580.J6K37   1997
222'.1109505—dc20
96-20807
CIP   AC

JOSEPH

AND HIS

COAT OF MANY COLORS

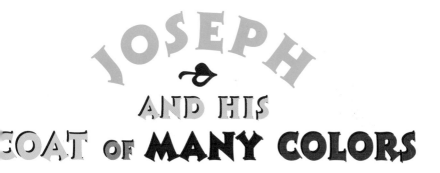

by Sue Kassirer
illustrated by Danuta Jarecka

Ready-to-Read
Aladdin Paperbacks

Jacob lived long ago.

He had twelve sons.

His favorite son was Joseph.

Jacob made Joseph
a coat of many colors.

Joseph's older brothers were jealous.

"It's not fair!" they said.

Joseph had a dream.
"The sun, the moon,
and eleven stars
all bowed down
to me,"
he told his
brothers.

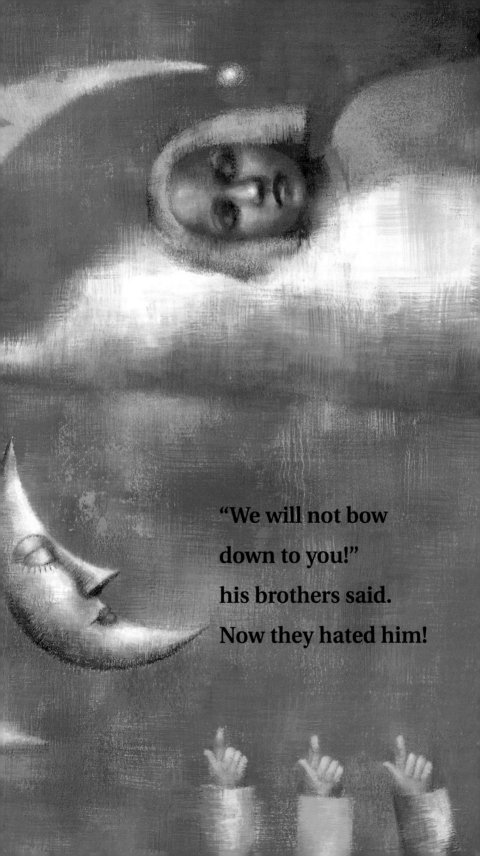

"We will not bow
down to you!"
his brothers said.
Now they hated him!

Joseph's brothers stole his coat.

They threw him in a pit.

Then they sold Joseph
to the Egyptians.

"A wild beast ate Joseph!"

the brothers told their father.

Jacob cried and cried.

Was Joseph really dead?

No!

He was alive in Egypt.

But he was in prison.

Joseph kept busy in prison.
He told the other prisoners
what their dreams meant.

Pharaoh was the king of Egypt.
One night he had
a scary dream.

What did the dream mean?
Everyone said, "Ask Joseph."

Pharaoh sent for Joseph.
"This was my dream," he said
"Seven thin cows ate
seven fat cows."

"Ah," said Joseph.
"God has spoken.
There will be seven
good years
and seven bad years.
You must store grain now
for the seven bad years."

"You are wise,"
said Pharaoh.

He asked Joseph
to help rule his land
and store the grain.

The seven good years ended.
They ended everywhere.
Joseph's brothers were hungry.
They heard about the
grain in Egypt.
"Let's go!" they said.

"We need to buy grain,"
they told Joseph.
They didn't know he was
their brother.
But Joseph knew who
they were!

Joseph was still angry
at his brothers.
What should he do?

Should he hurt his brothers?
Should he punish them?
Should he let them starve?
He could do anything—
anything he wanted!

Joseph thought hard.
He walked away
and cried.

Soon he came back.

"I am Joseph," he said.

He hugged his brothers.

Joseph's brothers were scared.

Was Joseph still angry?

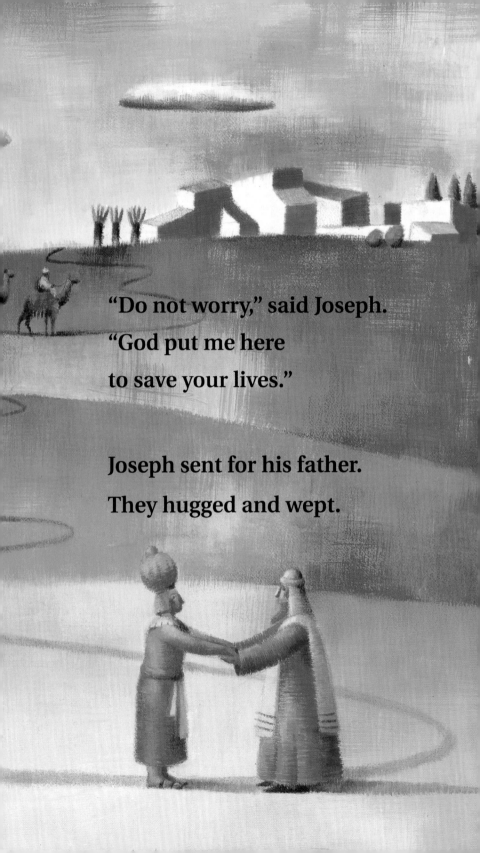

"Do not worry," said Joseph.
"God put me here
to save your lives."

Joseph sent for his father.
They hugged and wept.

Joseph gave his family
land and sheep.

Joseph forgave his brothers.
And he became a great ruler.